Library and Information Service

Library materials must be returned on or before the last date stamped or fines will be charged at the current rate. Items can be renewed online, by telephone, letter or personal call unless required by another borrower. For hours of opening and charges see notices displayed in libraries.

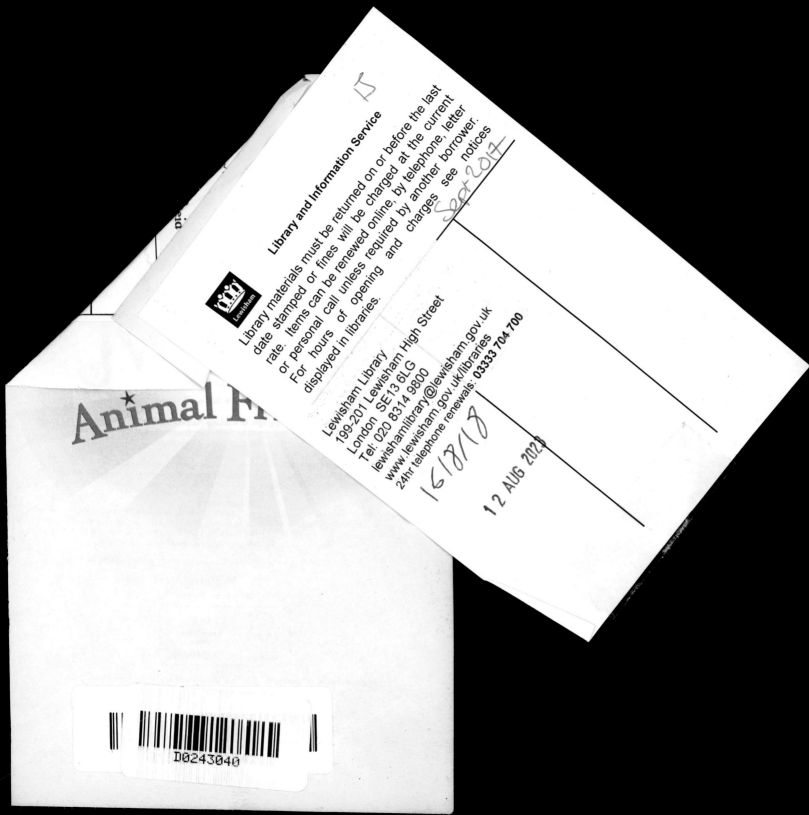

Lewisham Library
199-201 Lewisham High Street
London SE13 6LG
Tel: 020 8314 9800
lewishamlibrary@lewisham.gov.uk
www.lewisham.gov.uk/libraries
24hr telephone renewals: **03333 704 700**

Sept 2017

16/8/18

1 2 AUG 2020

15

Animal Fr

D0243040

For Hattie R

LEWISHAM
LIBRARY SERVICE

Askews & Holts	01-Sep-2017
JF SHORT CHAPTER	13

Special thanks to Valerie Wilding

ORCHARD BOOKS

First pub

Illustrations copyright © Working Partners Ltd 2017
Series created by Working Partners Ltd

The moral rights of the author and illustrator have been asserted.
All characters and events in this publication, other than those clearly in the public domain,
are fictitious and any resemblance to real persons, living or dead, is purely coincidental.

All rights reserved.
No part of this publication may be reproduced, stored in a retrieval system, or transmitted, in any form
or by any means, without the prior permission in writing of the publisher, nor be otherwise circulated in
any form of binding or cover other than that in which it is published and without a similar condition
including this condition being imposed on the subsequent purchaser.

A CIP catalogue record for this book is available from the British Library.

ISBN 978 1 40834 424 8

Printed in Great Britain

MIX
Paper from
responsible sources
FSC® C104740

The paper and board used in this book are made from wood from responsible sources

Orchard Books
An imprint of Hachette Children's Group
Part of The Watts Publishing Group Limited
Carmelite House, 50 Victoria Embankment, London EC4Y 0DZ

An Hachette UK Company
www.hachette.co.uk
www.hachettechildrens.co.uk

Ella Snugglepaw's Big Cuddle

Daisy Meadows

ORCHARD

Brighteyes' Home

Spelltop School

Treehouse

Picnic Area

Twinkling Inkwell

Sunshine Meadow

Honey Tree

Map of Friendship Forest

Library

Playground

Greenhouse

School Hall

Madame Doodleflap's House

Can you keep a secret? I thought you could!

Then I'll tell you about an enchanted wood.

It lies through the door in the old oak tree,

Let's go there now - just follow me!

We'll find adventure that never ends,

And meet the Magic Animal Friends!

Love,
Goldie the Cat

Contents

CHAPTER ONE

Snuggly Hugs

Lily Hart took a handful of curly kale leaves to her best friend, Jess Forester. "The guinea pigs will love this!" she said.

The girls were outside the Helping Paw Wildlife Hospital, which Lily's parents ran in a barn in their garden. Jess and her family lived right opposite Lily, and both

girls loved caring for the animal patients.
Today they were putting feed in the
outside runs where rabbits, guinea pigs,
squirrels and other creatures lived once
they were on the mend.

Jess's tabby kitten, Pixie, ran to meet
Mr Hart, who was bringing a bale of
straw for bedding. But then she spotted
something interesting in the hedge and
touched it with her little pink nose.

Lily went to have a look, too. "Pixie's
found a weird leafy thing hanging from a
twig," she called to the others.

"It's a chrysalis," Mr Hart said. "One

10

day it will become a butterfly."

"Wow!" said Jess, peering at the chrysalis too. It looked like a pea pod – green and closed up. When she touched it very gently, it was hard like a nut. "I can't believe a strange-looking thing like that can become something so beautiful!"

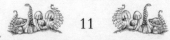

As Mr Hart headed for the stable, a flash
of gold among some roses caught Lily's
eye. "Look!" she called. "A butterfly!"

Jess grinned. "That's no butterfly. It's
Goldie!"

A beautiful cat with golden fur and eyes
as green as summer leaves ran to press
against their legs, purring. Goldie was
the girls' special friend. She took them on
amazing adventures in a magical place
called Friendship Forest, where all the
animals lived in little cottages or dens. And,
best of all, they could all talk!

Goldie suddenly darted towards

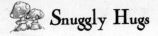

Brightley Stream, at the bottom of the garden.

"Come on!" said Jess. "She's taking us to Friendship Forest!"

They followed Goldie across the stream's stepping stones into Brightley Meadow, where a single bare tree stood. As Goldie drew near, it burst into life!

New leaves sprouted, uncurling to soak up the sun. Honeysuckle climbed through the branches, with bees buzzing among its sweetly scented flowers. In the grass below, wild strawberries glowed like red jewels beneath tall purple foxgloves. Pink-

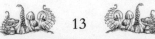

breasted chaffinches swooped through the
branches, chattering loudly to each other.

Lily squeezed Jess's hand. The
Friendship Tree!

Goldie touched it with her paw,
and two words
appeared in the
bark. "Friendship
Forest!"

When they read
the words aloud,
a door appeared
in the trunk! Lily
turned its leaf-

14

shaped handle and the door opened, spilling out golden light. This happened every time they went to Friendship Forest, but it always felt very special.

The cat leaped inside and the girls followed. They felt a familiar tingle, and knew it meant they were shrinking, just a little.

When the glow faded, Jess and Lily found themselves in a sun-dappled forest glade. The scent of candyfloss flowers drifted on the warm breeze. And there was Goldie, wearing her glittery scarf and standing almost as tall as their shoulders.

 15

She hugged them. "Jess! Lily!" she said in her soft voice. "Welcome to Friendship Forest."

"It's great to be back!" said Lily.

"And to talk to you!" Jess added. "Have you fetched us here because Grizelda's causing trouble again?"

Grizelda was a bad witch who wanted to get rid of all the animals in Friendship Forest so she could have it for herself. Goldie and the girls had always managed to stop her wicked plans, but their last adventure had left them feeling worried. Odd things had happened at Spelltop School, where all the little animals went. Even worse, one of the school's teachers, Professor Cutiepaws, had been acting strangely, and Jess and Lily suspected she was helping the witch.

Goldie shook her head. "Grizelda hasn't been around," she said, "and Professor

Cutiepaws hasn't done anything unusual.

But there is someone who needs help."

She pointed to a pretty brown and white

cow, standing beneath a mulberry tree.

"Hello!" the girls called.

The cow trotted over on dainty hooves.

Her big brown eyes were fringed by long

eyelashes, and she wore a pink and lilac

striped bag around her neck.

"Hello," the cow said. "Who are you?"

"These are my friends, Jess and Lily,"

said Goldie.

Jess smiled. "What's your name?"

"I can't remember," the cow said sadly.

 18

"Oh dear," Lily said. "How strange."

A furry, silver-grey face popped out of the cow's bag. "I know! I've been trying to jog her memory, but nothing's working …"

It was a little koala, with round fluffy ears, a dark nose and coppery eyes. She climbed out of the bag and jumped down.

"I'm Ella Snugglepaw," she said in a husky voice. "I met this lovely cow on my way to school."

"I'm Lily and this is Jess," said Lily. "Nice to meet you."

"Has she really forgotten her name?" Jess whispered to Ella. "That's awful."

"It's worse than that," the koala said. "She's forgotten everything – everything she ever knew!"

CHAPTER TWO

Bingo on Guard

The cow mooed sadly.

"Imagine having no memories," Jess whispered to Lily, "not even your name."

"We'll call you Miss Lovely," said Ella, "because that's what you are: lovely."

"If we can help you, Miss Lovely," said Lily, "we will."

Ella scrambled into Lily's arms. "Goldie said you'd help!" she cried, hugging her. Lily pressed her check against the koala's thick, silvery fur. It felt so soft!

Next it was Jess's turn for a hug. The little koala snuffled against her neck. Ella gave the nicest hugs.

Suddenly Jess had an idea. She grinned. "What about the Memory Tree? That helped us in our adventure with Hannah Honeypaw the bear."

Lily's eyes brightened, but Goldie shook

 22

her head. "Sorry, Jess," she said. "The Memory Tree only helps people when they need to remember something in particular. It can't help someone who's forgotten everything."

Lily knelt beside Miss Lovely. "Maybe there's a clue in your bag," she said.

The cow looked inside, pulled out a piece of paper and passed it to Lily. Everyone watched as she unfolded it.

"It's a map!" said Goldie, peering over Lily's shoulder. "It shows the way to Spelltop School. Is that where you were going, Miss Lovely?"

The cow's brown eyes swam with tears. "I can't remember." Lily tucked the map back in the bag and patted Miss Lovely's neck. "We'll take you to the school," she said. "It might jog your memory."

"Brilliant!" said Ella, jumping up and down. "Let's go!"

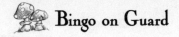

The friends arrived at the Spelltop School gate. Blossoms rambled over the buildings, which were made of woven branches. Swings, picnic tables and a treehouse dotted the grassy playground.

"KWARK!"

They looked up. An orb of light was speeding over the treetops towards them. A pink bird with a big curved beak followed close behind.

"KWARK!" he croaked.

"Oh no!" groaned Lily. "It's Grizelda's flamingo helper."

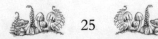

Jess held Ella close as the orb exploded into stinky sparks.

The witch appeared. She was wearing skinny black trousers, a purple tunic, spiky boots and a black cloak. The flamingo chick landed beside her on spindly legs.

"Go away, Grizelda," Jess shouted. "We won't let you succeed!"

"Ha!" Grizelda cackled. Her green hair whipped

around her head as she turned to the flamingo. "Bingo! Stop these girls interfering while I start my plan."

She dashed into the trees.

Jess passed Ella to Goldie. "Quick, Lily!" she yelled. "We have to stop her!"

The girls ran after Grizelda, but Bingo raced around them, trying to trip them up. He stuck out his tongue.

Then he turned cartwheels, making them leap aside in case he knocked them over.

"Heehee!" Bingo laughed. "Clever me!"

"You're mean, not clever," Lily shouted.

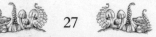

Jess clasped Lily's hand. "Walk slowly and ignore him."

Bingo turned another cartwheel, but his legs tangled and he flopped on the ground. Lily and Jess stepped around him, taking no notice.

"Horrible girls!" Bingo said crossly. He untangled his legs, muttering, "Nasty … ignoring me …!"

Once the girls were among the trees, they could see no sign of Grizelda.

Jess groaned. "The forest's so big – we'll never find her now!"

 28

CHAPTER THREE

Spell Class

Jess and Lily returned to the clearing to find Bingo gone and Miss Lovely sniffing at lazy daisies.

"Grizelda got away," Jess said. "Now what do we do?"

Ella hugged the girls. Her warm, snuggly cuddle instantly made them

feel a bit better.

"Let's take Miss Lovely into the school," Ella suggested. "She might recognise something. Or someone."

"Good idea," said Lily. "Come on, Miss Lovely." They all walked into the school.

Miss Lovely looked around the cloakroom. "I don't remember this," she said. She didn't remember the pictures on the walls, either.

"Let's try the spell room," Ella suggested. "My class will be there. Maybe someone will recognise Miss Lovely."

The girls peered through the window

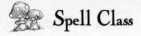

in the classroom door. The spell room was
lined with potion bottles and jars. Bowls
of leaves, berries and toadstools stood
on shelves above a stack of cauldrons.
There was a whiteboard on the wall, with
"Spells must Rhyme!" written in blue.

The teacher was a beautiful fluffy
white cat with a pink bow.

"Professor Cutiepaws!" said Jess.

"Let's ask if she knows a spell to bring Miss Lovely's memory back," said Ella.

"We'd better not," Lily whispered. "We don't know if we can trust her."

Professor Cutiepaws was always very nice, but everything seemed to go wrong when she was around. At first, the girls had thought it was just Professor Cutiepaws's clumsiness … but then they had begun to suspect that she was messing things up on purpose because she was helping Grizelda.

"This could be a test!" Jess said. "If

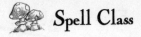

Professor Cutiepaws helps us, we'll know she's as nice as she seems."

As they slipped into the classroom, all the little animals wriggled excitedly.

"Remember, sweetiepies," Professor Cutiepaws said, "spells … must … rhyme." She pointed a pen at the board and a red line magically appeared beneath each word.

"Hello, everyone," said Lily.

Professor Cutiepaws whirled around, dropping the pen. Her white fur stood on end.

The class all giggled. Professor

Ella Snugglepaw

Cutiepaws was so clumsy!

A smile stretched across the cat's face. "Silly me!" she said. "I was shocked – I mean, surprised – to see you. Ella, too!"

"Sorry I'm late," said the koala.

"It doesn't matter, sugarplum," cooed Professor Cutiepaws. Then she frowned. "What's that cow doing here?"

"She's lost her memory," Jess explained. "We thought you'd know a spell to bring it back."

Professor Cutiepaws backed away. "Sorry, sweetiekins, but I have to teach my lesson right now."

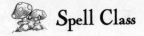

"Can we stay?" asked Lily. "Maybe you could help afterwards."

The cat smiled her widest smile. "Of course."

"You're so kind," said Ella. "Have a hug!"

The smile vanished. Professor Cutiepaws froze as Ella flung her arms around her.

"She's not enjoying that hug," Goldie whispered.

"Then there's definitely

something wrong," said Jess. "Ella's hugs
are the best!"

"And she isn't pleased to see us," said
Lily. "Her fur went as bristly as a brush!"

Professor Cutiepaws unpeeled Ella's
paws, and the koala went to sit next to
Molly Twinkletail the mouse.

Jess, Lily and Goldie settled in the book
corner.

"My disappearing spell will get rid of
all the nasty weeds in Friendship Forest,"
Professor Cutiepaws told the class. "I've
just invented it. Aren't I brilliantly clever?
This is how it works."

 36

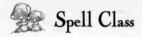

She heaped some straggly weeds on her table and chanted.

"*Power of mould and slime and grit,*

Magic spell, work bit by bit.

Make my table nice and clear,

Weedy weeds – disappear!"

The straggly heap vanished in a puff of cheesy-smelling smoke.

"Wow!" said Molly.

"Fantastic!" cried Sophie Flufftail the squirrel.

"Hooray!" cheered Emily Prickleback

the hedgehog. "We can get rid of all the weeds in our forest!"

Jess wasn't so sure. "That spell sounds useful," she whispered to Lily, "but I don't trust Professor Cutiepaws."

As the cat piled weeds in front of each excited animal, Miss Lovely joined Goldie and the girls.

"Ready, honeybuns?" Professor Cutiepaws pointed her pen at the board, and the words of the spell appeared. Then she sat at her table. "We'll chant the spell together, and when your weeds disappear, so will all the ones in the forest!"

 38

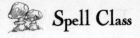

"Oooh!" said the little animals.

The chanting began.

"*Power of mould and slime and grit,*

Magic spell, work bit by bit.

Make the forest nice and clear,

Weedy weeds – disappear."

The weeds vanished amid puffs of cheesy smoke. But there was a bigger puff in the book corner. When the smoke cleared, the girls gasped. Miss Lovely had vanished, too!

The girls gasped in horror.

Professor Cutiepaws clapped her paws to her cheeks in dismay. "How did that

 39

happen?" she cried. "You silly animals must have said the spell wrong."

"We didn't," sobbed Mia Floppyear the bunny. "Our weeds disappeared!"

Soon the whole class was wailing.

"Do stop, my treasures!" said Professor Cutiepaws, as Ella ran around comforting

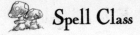

everyone with hugs.

Lily glanced at Jess. "It wasn't the class that did this to Miss Lovely," she said. "Professor Cutiepaws is acting strangely. I think she's up to something."

"Let's take a look at that spell," said Jess.

While Professor Cutiepaws was shushing the animals, Goldie and the girls went to Professor Cutiepaws's table. There was an open notebook on it. The friends scanned the words and gasped. It sounded like the first spell, but the words were very different.

"*Make my new home nice and clear,*

 41

Horrid forest – disappear.

One more thing must go right now.

Get rid of that pesky cow."

Jess pointed at Professor Cutiepaws.
"You did it!" she shouted. "You said
this spell instead! You're working for
Grizelda!"

Professor Cutiepaws burst into loud
sobs. "You're being terribly mean to me! I
didn't change that spell. I'm NOT helping
Grizelda!" she said. "And that's the truth."

Then, with a flick of her fluffy tail, she
ran from the room.

CHAPTER FOUR

Professor Wiggly's Library

"After her!" said Lily. "Ella, stay here. If Professor Cutiepaws is helping Grizelda, she could be dangerous."

Ella clung to Jess's leg. "Please let me come," she begged. "I want to help find Miss Lovely!"

The girls hesitated, then nodded to each other. Ella had found Miss Lovely the first time, and she deserved to help them find her again.

"OK," said Jess. "But you'll have to hold on tight." She scooped Ella into her arms and raced outside with Lily and Goldie.

"KWARK!"

Bingo stood on the gatepost.

"Ignore him again," Lily said, reaching for the latch.

But Bingo flapped his wings so hard she had to cover her eyes against the swirling dust that flew up.

44

"Heeheehee!"
he laughed. "You can't
ignore me now."

"Bully!" Goldie shouted,
shielding Lily with a protective
paw. "Bullies just want attention, so we'll
take no notice."

They turned their backs on Bingo.

"We'll never find Professor Cutiepaws
now," Jess said. "Let's go to the school
library. Maybe Professor Wiggly the
bookworm can find a spell that might
help."

Ella Snugglepaw

The girls, Goldie, and Ella made their way to the library. It was a big room lined with books from floor to ceiling. There were lots of cosy nooks filled with colourful stools and squashy red cushions.

Professor Wiggly looked up from his desk. "Visitors! Lovely!" he said. "I was

 just writing some titles in my *Book of Books*." Seeing the worry on Goldie's face, his smile

vanished. "What's wrong?"

"Ella found a lost cow," said Goldie. "All she had was a bag with this map in it." She showed it to Professor Wiggly.

"Well, that's all right," he said. "You showed her the way! What's the problem?"

"The cow had completely lost her memory," said Lily. "Then Professor Cutiepaws said a spell that made her disappear."

"Poor Professor Cutiepaws," said Professor Wiggly with a sigh. "She's always having accidents like this."

The girls glanced at each other. Were

they really accidents?

"Professor, is there a spell in one of your books that could make the cow reappear?" asked Lily.

"Hmm," said the bookworm. He picked up his long golden bookmark and swept it along a shelf labelled "Magic".

They watched in amazement as a whole row of books floated down onto his desk. He began checking the indexes.

"Any luck?" Lily asked after a while.

"Not so far," he replied, and kept looking.

"Hmm," he said finally. "Sorry, but it

seems there simply is no reappearing spell."

Goldie's whiskers drooped. "Now what?"

Ella hugged her. "Cheer up!" she said. "Maybe someone can make a new spell?"

"Only witches can create new spells," Professor Wiggly said sadly.

"Then let's ask Grizelda really nicely," Ella said, her eyes wide and eager. "I'm sure she'd help."

Jess tickled Ella's fluffy ear. "That's a sweet idea," she said, "but Grizelda will never help us. She's too mean."

 49

Professor Wiggly opened a tin and offered some raspberry buns to the friends. "I wish we knew a good witch."

Jess nearly dropped her bun in excitement. "Oh, but we do! We helped some small witches get away from Grizelda. They guard the Heart Trees now."

The four Heart Trees were named Laughter, Sweet Dreams, Memory and Kindness. Each held ancient magic that helped the

animals in the Forest.

"The Memory Tree is near here," said
Goldie.

"Thistle guards that one," said Lily.
"She'll help us!"

Ella clapped her paws in excitement, but
suddenly she stopped.

There were squawks and squeals coming
from outside, as if all the animals in the
forest were crying out for help.

The friends ran to the window. Birds
circled frantically overhead, cawing,
while below a family of squirrels huddled
together by a huge birch tree. They

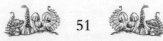

watched in horror as the tree suddenly
disappeared in a puff of yellow-green
smoke. The panicked squirrel family
bounded away into the forest.

"Did you see that?" Lily cried. "A
whole tree just vanished!"

"That's why the birds and animals are
so upset," Goldie said in dismay. "Their
trees have vanished, too!"

"We've got to get help!" said Jess. "And
fast, before the whole forest is gone!"

CHAPTER FIVE

A Ball of Purple Light

As the friends raced through the forest, they saw plants, trees and flowers disappearing left and right. Clumps of grass vanished, leaving bare earth behind. A haze of cheesy smoke hung in the air.

Lily stopped suddenly. "Agatha Glitterwing the magpie lived here," she

said, pointing to a bare spot. "Her tree's gone! Where will she live now?"

The tree where Captain Ace the stork tethered his hot air balloon had vanished too. The balloon was floating away into the sky.

Ella shivered. "We'll fix this, won't we?"

Jess held Ella tight. "We'll try our very best," she said.

In Toadstool Glade, Mr and Mrs Longwhiskers the rabbits stood where their café had been. Tears ran down their faces.

Ella hurried to hug them.

 54

"We'll get help," Lily promised the rabbits. "We'll try to make everything all right."

Mrs Longwhiskers smiled bravely. "We know you will." She turned to Ella. "Thank you for the lovely hugs."

The friends hurried on.

"Grizelda must have made Professor Cutiepaws cast that disappearing spell," said Jess as they ran. "She's getting rid of

 55

everything in the forest. Soon the animals will have nowhere to live and they'll have to leave."

Lily nodded grimly. "She'll fill Friendship Forest with creepers and swamps."

"Here's the Heart Path!" cried Goldie. "Nearly there!"

They breathed a sigh of relief when the huge Memory Tree came into sight with its key-shaped leaves and clusters of delicate yellow flowers hanging from every branch.

"Thank goodness it hasn't disappeared,"

 56

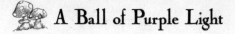

panted Lily as they ran.

Nearby, a small witch bobbed around on her broomstick. She was about the same age as the girls, and she wore a green skirt with long striped socks. Her hair was an untidy mass of purple curls.

"Oopsy woopsy!" she cried as she made a wobbly landing in a nearby oak tree.

Jess grinned. "Thistle never was a good flyer!"

The witch shook her scruffy hair out of her eyes and saw the friends. "What's happening?" she cried. "Everything's disappearing!"

Ella Snugglepaw

As she spoke, the oak tree vanished. Thistle tumbled to the ground.

"Oopsy woopsy!" She sat rubbing her knees.

The little koala scurried to her. "I'm Ella," she said. "Would you like a hug?"

"It might make me feel better," said the small witch, her lower lip trembling.

Ella jumped into her lap and hugged her.

Thistle smiled. "I do feel better!"

"That's

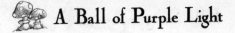

good," said Jess. "Because we need your help. New spells can only be made by a witch, and we need a new spell! Could you create one to make everything reappear? A missing cow, too?"

"Ooh, I'm not clever enough for that," said Thistle.

Ella hugged her tightly. "You are!"

"Well … I'll try!" said Thistle. She concentrated, screwing up her little face.

The friends waited and worried as every few moments another tree or plant disappeared in a puff of nasty, cheesy-smelling smoke.

Goldie twisted her tail anxiously.

Suddenly, Thistle grinned. "I've got it. A spell to bring things back!"

"And the cow?" said Lily.

"Oh!" Thistle concentrated again, then said, "Ready! We'll know it's worked when a ball of purple light appears – that's the magic!"

She held out her hands, palms up. "Here goes," she said.

"*Purple light, ride on the breeze.*

Bring back buildings, plants and trees.

Make them reappear right now

And the cow must come back too."

 60

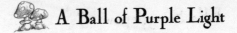

Everyone waited, holding their breath.

Nothing happened.

"What went wrong?" Thistle wondered.

"Maybe it's because the last line didn't rhyme," Lily suggested. "Professor Cutiepaws said rhyming's important."

"I knew I wasn't clever enough," Thistle wailed.

"Of course you are. Let's just change the words around," Jess suggested. She took out the little sketchbook and pencil she always carried and gave it to the small witch.

Thistle chewed the pencil. "What

rhymes with 'now'?" she asked. "There's 'how' and 'bow' ..."

"'Wow'?" Goldie offered.

"Why not 'cow'?" said Lily.

"Of course!" Jess took the pencil and wrote quickly.

Thistle watched, grinning. "That should work!"

"Hooray!" Ella sang.

Thistle opened her hands and chanted.

"Purple light, ride on the breeze.

Bring back buildings, plants and trees.

Make them reappear right now

And bring back our lovely friend the cow!"

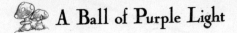

A ball of shimmering purple light
formed in Thistle's hands.

Everyone gasped.

"Fantastic!" said Jess.

"Brilliant!" said Goldie.

Thistle looked pleased. "Now I have to
fly really high," she said, "and spread the
light across the forest."

She climbed on to her broom,
balancing the ball of light on one hand.
Then she glanced over the girls' shoulders
and squealed in fright.

Jess and Lily spun around. Bingo the
flamingo was zooming towards Thistle,

flinging pine cones at her.

Thistle tried to dodge them, but she wobbled and fell off her broomstick.

"Oopsy woopsy!" She rolled on the ground, still clutching the ball of light.

Goldie shielded Ella while Jess and Lily threw clumps of moss at Bingo, yelling, "Leave her alone!"

Bingo swooped down, snatched up the

 64

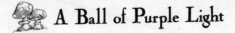

broomstick and banged it against the
Memory Tree.

Crack!

It broke in half.

Thistle burst into tears.

"Hah!" shouted Bingo. "Your witch
friend can't fly now, so she can't cast her
silly spell. Heeheehee! You'll never stop
Grizelda's plan!"

He flew off.

"He's gone," said Jess, "and soon
everything in the forest will be gone, too."
No sooner had she finished speaking than
a nearby Twisty Willow vanished.

"I'm sorry," Thistle said, sniffling. "I can't fly high and spread the light without my broomstick."

Ella's fluffy cheeks were damp with tears, too, and Goldie's whiskers drooped as she picked up the trembling koala.

"We'll think of something, won't we?" Ella said.

"Of course," Lily replied, forcing a note of cheer into her voice. She glanced at Jess's worried face, and whispered, "But I don't know what."

CHAPTER SIX

Bouncing Bingo

"Thistle, why not climb the Memory Tree?" Jess suggested. "Then you could throw the orb and let the wind spread it!"

"I'm too clumsy to climb so high," the small witch replied. "I'd fall."

"I'll climb it," Ella said firmly. "Koalas are great climbers, and I'm very light, so

I can climb the thinner branches at the top."

She asked Goldie for Miss Lovely's bag and Thistle put the ball of light inside. Then she scrambled up the tree, arm over arm, higher and higher.

"KWARK!"

Bingo the flamingo suddenly reappeared. He circled the Memory Tree before landing on a branch. Then he bounced up and down, shaking it.

"You horrid bird!" cried Jess. "Get away!"

He bounced harder.

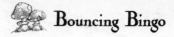

Ella shrieked as she flew into the air. She grabbed a branch and held tight, crying, "Stop him! I'll fall!"

Jess started climbing up to help Ella, but Bingo just bounced her off.

"What can we do?" Lily said helplessly.

As she spoke, a

whole copse of hazelnut trees vanished.
Harsh sunshine flooded the ground,
instead of the lovely dappled sunlight
everyone loved so much.

"Jess! Lily!" Ella cried. "Suppose the
Memory Tree vanishes while I'm in it!"

"We'd catch you!" Jess shouted.

"You wouldn't!" Bingo squawked.

"Ignore him, Ella!" Lily shouted
through cupped hands. "Think positively!"

"Hold tight when he bounces," yelled
Jess. "Imagine giving the tree your best
hug."

Ella squeezed her eyes closed and

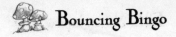

hugged the trunk.

Bingo bounced again and again but soon realised he couldn't shake Ella off. He stuck out his tongue at her and flew away with one last "KWARK!"

"He's gone!" Thistle yelled.

Ella opened her eyes.

"You're such a brave koala," Lily called.

"With the best, tightest hugs!" Jess added.

Ella scurried up the tree as quickly as she could. "I'm at the top!" she called finally.

"Throw the ball of light as high as you

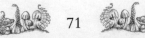

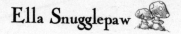

can!" Thistle told her.

The magic ball soared into the air.
The breeze caught it, and it burst into a
thousand sparkles of light, which blew in
every direction.

Jess and Lily couldn't believe their
eyes! Flowers, bushes and trees magically
reappeared all around. So did the animals'
little cottages, nestling among tree roots,
or high in the branches.

Ella scrambled down and hugged
everyone, then hugged them all again as
they laughed and cheered.

"Thistle's spell worked!" Lily said.

"Thanks to Ella," Thistle said happily.

"Now the forest is back to normal," said Jess, "maybe Miss Lovely's back, too. Let's go to Spelltop School and see."

They ran through the forest, laughing as starflower bushes popped up alongside the path. Sunshine Meadow was full of flowers, and everywhere looked beautiful again. In Toadstool Glade, Mr and Mrs Longwhiskers hopped with happiness to see their café back.

"Thanks, everyone!" they called.

As the friends reached Spelltop School, they were overjoyed to find Miss Lovely wandering around near the gate. She mooed softly as Ella hugged her and gave her the striped bag.

"Is this mine?" Miss Lovely asked.

Lily's heart sank. The cow's memory hadn't come back.

"Can you remember anything?" she asked.

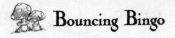

Miss Lovely shook her head sadly. "Nothing."

Ella had an idea. "Maybe the reappearing spell could bring the cow's memory back?"

"It might if I change the words," said Thistle. "Jess, can I borrow your book and pencil again?"

Thistle wrote, crossed out and wrote again. Finally, she said, "I've got it – here goes.

"Purple light upon the breeze
That brought back buildings, plants and trees.
In addition to all of these,

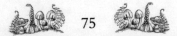

Bring back the cow's lost memories."

The girls held their breath. A ball of shimmering purple light appeared in Thistle's hands.

"It worked!" Lily and Jess cried together.

Thistle threw the orb into the air and it shattered into sparkling purple raindrops that rained down upon Miss Lovely.

"Ooh!" mooed the cow. Her eyes brightened. "I'm starting to remember …"

Ella bounced up and down. "Remember what?"

The cow laughed. "Everything!"

CHAPTER SEVEN

A Special Assembly

"My name is Professor Poppycud!" the cow said happily. "I travelled from far across the forest to be Spelltop School's new teacher. On my way, I met a white cat wearing a pink bow."

Jess gasped. "Professor Cutiepaws!"

"What happened?" asked Ella, who was

hugging the cow's leg tightly.

"She said she'd told Professor Gogglewing I wasn't coming," said Professor Poppycud. "She was taking my place at Spelltop so she could steal Professor Wiggly's special books! Then she started chanting and I forgot everything I ever knew."

"That proves it! Professor Cutiepaws is helping Grizelda!" said Lily. "She's using her bad spells!"

Ella stared. "Our teacher's working for a witch?"

Jess nodded. "And when Professor

 78

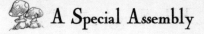

Poppycud came to school today, Professor Cutiepaws made her disappear in case Professor Gogglewing saw her and discovered the truth."

Goldie suddenly jumped. "Eeoww!" she yelped, rubbing her head and looking down at the ground. "Someone's throwing acorns!"

They ducked behind the school gate.

"Heeheehee!"

Bingo was circling overhead. He blew a raspberry and flung more acorns.

"Bingo, why are you helping Grizelda?" Lily shouted.

"Because she'll give me an amazing reward if I do!" He blew another raspberry. "Thhhbbpp!"

"Grizelda never keeps her promises!" yelled Jess.

Bingo landed on a tree stump and cocked his head. "That's not true at all!"

"Yes, it is," Lily said. "Ask anyone who's ever helped her!"

"They're right," added Goldie. "She's

80

promised her helpers all kinds of things —
treats, a new home, a boat — but she never
gives them anything, because she only
cares about herself."

"Is that true?" Bingo asked, looking
worried.

They nodded. "What did Grizelda
promise you?" asked Jess.

The flamingo's neck drooped. "My
brothers, Banjo, Cosmo and Gonzo,
always ignore me." He sniffed. "So
Grizelda promised to be my friend. But
she's always shouting at me."

Ella scampered to Bingo. "I'll be your

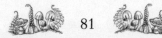

friend," she said. "Would you like a hug?"

Bingo nodded. "I think I would."

Ella smiled and threw her arms around him. He looked as if he didn't know what to do at first, but then he curled his neck around the koala and closed his eyes.

After a moment, Bingo straightened up. "I'm sorry for being horrible," he said. "I'm glad the cow's back. I heard

Professor Cutiepaws created a spell to make her disappear."

Lily stared. "She made that spell? Not Grizelda?"

"Professor Wiggly said only witches can create spells!" cried Jess.

"So that means …" Goldie began.

Ella was horrified. "Professor Cutiepaws is just like Grizelda – she's a witch!"

"Hello!" said a voice.

It was Professor Gogglewing the goose. "Isn't it marvellous that the forest is back to normal? Bingo, why not come and join your brothers in school?" His eyes landed

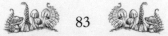

on the cow. "Why, Professor Poppycud!" he cried. "Professor Cutiepaws told us you were too unwell! That's why you sent her in your place!"

Goldie's whiskers twitched. "Professor, we'll explain everything. But first, where's Professor Cutiepaws?"

"In the hall, starting our special assembly," he replied. "It's to reward all the pupils who have tried their hardest."

"Wait!" cried

Lily. "We have something to tell you!"

The girls and Goldie filled Professor Gogglewing in on how Professor Cutiepaws was helping Grizelda.

"You see?" Jess finished. "She's a witch, too!"

The elderly goose was horrified. "We must stop her!" he cried. "Who knows what she'll do next?"

Everyone raced to the hall, with Bingo flying above. Jess opened the door a crack. All the little animals sat before Professor Cutiepaws, with their parents sitting proudly behind them.

 85

Professor Cutiepaws beamed. "I've something special for all you lovelies!"

The pupils shared excited glances as Professor Cutiepaws's voice rang out.

"*Power of mould and slime and grit,*

Magic spell, work bit by bit."

Jess turned to the others in alarm. "The disappearing spell!"

Professor Cutiepaws chanted on:

"*Make the forest nice and clear,*

Little creatures—"

Jess and Lily burst into the hall, shouting, "STOP!"

Bingo flew at Professor Cutiepaws,

 86

who swiped at him

with her paws and

shrieked.

The watching

pupils and parents

looked on, stunned.

"She's trying to make all you animals

disappear!" cried Lily.

The little ones squealed and scurried to

their frightened parents, while Jess pointed

at Professor Cutiepaws. "You're a witch,

just like Grizelda!"

The animals looked from the girls to

Professor Cutiepaws, unsure of what to

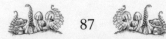

do.

"Thistle!" Lily whispered. "Can you think of a spell that will show everyone the truth?"

"But what?" Thistle looked panicky. "Ooh, I can't think!"

"Try to write it down!" said Jess, whipping out her sketchbook and handing it to Thistle, who scribbled a few words. Jess pointed to one and whispered in her ear.

Then Thistle started chanting.

"Purple light upon the breeze

That brought back buildings, plants and trees.

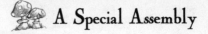

We don't believe this cat is real

If she's a witch, then please – reveal!"

A purple orb appeared in Thistle's

hands and she threw it towards Professor

Cutiepaws. It burst against her white fur

in a shower of stinking yellow sparks and

purple smoke. Frightened, the girls closed

their eyes and backed away. After a few

moments, Lily eased her eyes open and

gasped.

"Jess, look!" she cried.

The smoke had cleared, and Professor

Cutiepaws was gone. In her place stood a

tall woman with wiry hair, skinny black

 89

trousers, a purple tunic, spiky boots and a black cloak like bat wings.

Grizelda!

The witch's green hair, which still had a pink bow in it, crackled and her eyes widened in shock.

The animals sat frozen.

"She's not a witch like Grizelda," Lily said, astonished. "Professor Cutiepaws *is* Grizelda!"

CHAPTER EIGHT

Reward Roses

Goldie glared. "Grizelda, it was you all along!"

Grizelda sneered. "Turning myself into Miss sickly-sweet Cutiepaws was so clever!"

Professor Poppycud mooed right in the witch's face. "These girls are too clever

for you, Grizelda!"

Professor Gogglewing pointed to the door. "Out!"

Grizelda shook her fist. "I'm glad I'm leaving," she screeched. "I hated being nice to you nasty animals, with your silly squeaks and giggles – ugh!"

Her face turned purple as she pulled the
pink bow from her hair and snarled, "I'll
create another, more brilliant plan – one
you girls won't be able to ruin! You'd ALL
better watch out." She glared at Bingo as
she stomped towards the door. "Come on,
Bingo!"

He didn't move.

"I said, come on!" Grizelda shouted.

Bingo stuck his beak in the air. "No!"

"What?" screeched the witch.

"You should try being nice, not nasty,"
said Bingo. "A hug might help." He strode
over to Grizelda, and wrapped his wings

around her.

The witch pushed him away. "Hugs are disgusting!" she shrieked. She turned to Jess, Lily and Goldie. "You're all disgusting!"

But they just laughed.

"You wait!" Grizelda cried. "I'll be back! Friendship Forest will be mine!"

She snapped her fingers and disappeared in a spatter of smelly sparks.

Professor Gogglewing flapped the sparks away. "What a to-do!" he said. "Thank you, Lily, Jess and Goldie. You've protected our school once more."

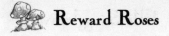

Lily smiled. "We couldn't have done it without Ella. She kept us all feeling positive."

"And gave lovely hugs!" Jess grinned.

The headmaster smiled at the koala. "Thank you, Ella! Let's start the assembly," he said, picking up his basket. "Then we'll all have raspberry fizz and cherry cookies to welcome our new teacher, Professor Poppycud!"

There were cheers for the cow, whose eyelashes fluttered like paper fans!

Professor Gogglewing presented silver roses to animals who had tried their

hardest, especially when they found work difficult.

"Next," he said, "some special roses. Charlotte Waggytail!"

The little puppy bounded up to receive a golden rose for showing other animals what fun reading was.

The girls clapped hard. They'd shared a magical adventure with Charlotte!

Another friend, Layla Brighteye the meerkat, was next. Her golden rose was for painting pictures to decorate the school walls.

A sweet little kitten called Ava

 96

Fluffyface, who the girls had met on their last adventure, received a golden rose for helping to fill the forest with music.

"The fourth Reward Rose," said Professor Gogglewing, "goes to Ella Snugglepaw, who brings a positive attitude to everything. And hugs!"

Everyone clapped, then the headmaster said, "I've got one more golden rose for someone brave enough to stand up to a bully. Bingo Pinkbill tried to show Grizelda that she could be nice if she wanted. Come on up, Bingo!"

"Go, Bingo!" his brother Gonzo cried, amid huge cheers.

"Yay! Bingo!" cried Cosmo.

"You're the best!" shouted Banjo.

Bingo flapped his wings happily. He'd gone from having no friends to having a whole school full of friends, including his brothers! Bingo smiled

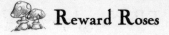

as he came forward to accept his golden
rose, holding it in his beak.

Jess and Lily heard a tap on the door
and peeped out to see two tall flamingos.
Their wings fluttered anxiously.

"We're the Pinkbills," said one. "We've
been searching for our four missing chicks.
Then Professor Gogglewing sent us a flyer
inviting us here."

"We wondered why," Mrs Pinkbill
added.

Lily threw the door wide. "This is why!"

Bingo flew at them. "Mum! Dad!"

Banjo, Cosmo and Gonzo scrambled

to greet their parents. The whole Pinkbill family disappeared among flapping wings and happy croaks.

"A witch took us away!" said Bingo.

"We didn't know how to get back," added Cosmo.

"We've made friends," Banjo said.

"Can we stay?" begged Gonzo.

The Pinkbills looked at Professor Gogglewing, who said, "We've plenty of room at school, and we love to include new friends."

"I don't know ... We're a long way from Paradise Ponds," said Mr Pinkbill.

"But your chicks all love going to our school," said Professor Gogglewing. "If you move here, I promise you'll feel right at home."

Mrs Pinkbill gazed at her chicks, "Well, if you're sure you want us all to stay …"

"Yes!" they cried. "Hooray!"

Professor Gogglewing smiled. "Raspberry fizz and cherry cookies for everyone!"

After the party ended, it was time for Jess and Lily to leave.

It took ages to say goodbye to all their animal friends, but finally they reached the gate.

"One more hug," said Ella. "Promise you'll come back soon?"

They promised! With a final wave, the girls followed Goldie through the forest to the Friendship Tree.

Jess hugged her. "Fetch us next time Grizelda causes trouble," she said.

"Of course!" Goldie said, giving Lily a hug.

She touched the tree trunk. A door opened, and golden light streamed out.

 102

Jess and Lily waved and stepped into the light. They felt the tingle that meant they were returning to their proper size.

When the light faded, they were back in Brightley Meadow. They ran across the stream and up the garden to where Pixie was snoozing by the hedge.

Lily looked at the chrysalis. It was moving!

"I think it's hatching!" she whispered.

They watched as a beautiful butterfly broke its way free from the chrysalis. A few moments later, its wings fluttered, and the girls glimpsed its brilliant red, brown

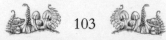

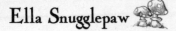

and white colours.

"It's lovely!" said

Jess. "Just think, we watched Professor

Cutiepaws change into something nasty –

Grizelda!"

"And now we've watched a caterpillar

change into something beautiful," said

Lily. "A butterfly!"

Jess grinned. "I wonder what surprise

Friendship Forest will have for us next

time!"

The End

In the magical land of Friendship Forest,
Lily and Jess are going to an Ice Show! But wicked
Grizelda is planning to spoil their special day
with a nasty spell.

Can adorable penguin Isla Waddlewing help
save Snowdrop Slopes from melting away?

Find out in the next Magic Animal Friends book,

Isla Waddlewing Breaks the Ice

Turn over for a sneak peek ...

"Finished!" said Lily Hart, brushing snow from her gloves.

Lily's best friend, Jess Forester, admired their snowman. "I think he's the best we've ever made!"

Jess was right. The snowman, made of three big balls of tightly packed snow, stood almost as tall as the girls. They couldn't stop grinning, though their fingers and toes tingled with cold.

Snow lay like a soft white blanket all around them, and the garden of the Helping Paw Wildlife Hospital was peaceful and silent. Lily's parents had brought the animals into the barn, where it was cosy and warm.

"Now for the finishing touches," said Jess. She added a row of little pebbles to the snowman's face, to make a smile. Then Lily found two bigger pebbles for the eyes.

"There's just one thing missing ..." said Lily, thoughtfully.

"A nose," said both girls at once. They looked at each other and laughed.

"What shall we use?" said Jess.

"I bet we can find something in the garden," said Lily. "Let's have a look."

The girls set off, boots sinking deep in

the snow as they explored the garden.

"I can't see a thing but white!" said Jess. "Except – what's that?"

She pointed to a flash of gold beneath a snow-laden bush.

"It's Goldie!" said Jess.

Sure enough, a golden cat strolled out from among the leaves, and shook snow from her fur. The girls' old friend waved her tail in the air, and let out a soft miaow.

"Are we going back to Friendship Forest?" asked Jess eagerly. Friendship Forest was a magical secret world where all the animals could talk and lived in adorable little cottages. Their friend Goldie had taken them on many adventures there.

As if in reply, Goldie set off, leaping through the snow and leaving neat little pawprints behind her.

Read

Isla Waddlewing Breaks the Ice

to find out what happens next!

Magic
Animal Friends

Can Jess and Lily save the magic of Friendship Forest from Grizelda? Read all of series seven to find out!

COMING SOON!
Look out for
Jess and Lily's
next adventure:
Isla Waddlewing Breaks the Ice!

3 stories in 1!

www.magicanimalfriends.com

Jess and Lily's Animal Facts

Lily and Jess love lots of different animals –
both in Friendship Forest
and in the real world.

Here are their top facts about

KOALAS

like Ella Snugglepaw:

- Koalas are mostly nocturnal, which means they sleep for part of the night and part of the daytime. They can sleep for up to 18-20 hours each day

- Baby koalas are called joeys

- Koalas eat about one kilogram of eucalyptus leaves a day. Eucalyptus leaves have a lot of moisture in them, so koalas do not need to drink much water

- In Aborigine language, the word 'koala' means 'no water'

- Koalas can store snacks of leaves in pouches in their cheeks

- Koalas are excellent swimmers. They have adapted to be able to cross rivers and escape from heavy flooding

Magic
Animal Friends
Can you keep the secret?

There's lots of fun for everyone at
www.magicanimalfriends.com

Play games and explore the secret world of
Friendship Forest, where animals can talk!

Join the
Magic Animal Friends Club!

⭐ Special competitions ⭐
⭐ Exclusive content ⭐
⭐ All the latest Magic Animal Friends news! ⭐

To join the Club, simply go to

www.magicanimalfriends.com/join-our-club/

Terms and Conditions
(1) Open to UK and Republic of Ireland residents only (2) Please get the email of your parent/guardian to enter
(3) We may use your data to contact you with further offers

Full terms and conditions at www.hachettechildrensdigital.co.uk/terms/